The Fourth Little Pig

by Teresa Celsi
illustrated by Doug Cushman

METROPOLITAN TEACHING AND LEARNING COMPANY

Metropolitan Teaching and Learning Company
33 Irving Place
NY, NY 10003

ISBN: 1-58120-900-2
This book also available in Big Book format. ISBN: 1-58120-118-4

10 9 8 7 6 5 4 3 2 1

The Fourth Little Pig

A long time ago,
There were three little pigs

4

A big bad wolf tried
To catch them one day,
By huffing and puffing
Two houses away.

6

Pig One and Pig Two
Then needed to flee.
They ran quickly to get
To the house of Pig Three.

They bolted the windows
And locked the front door.
"We won't go outside," they said.
"Not anymore."

They stayed in that house
At the top of the hill,

And those three silly pigs
Would be hiding there still—

If their traveling sister,
The daring Pig Four,
Hadn't stopped by to visit
And knocked on their door.

The door opened a crack.
Then it opened up wide.
"Quick! Get in," said the boys.
"There are bad wolves outside."

"Oh, pooh," said Pig Four,
"There are no wolves in sight."
"Yes, there are!" said her brothers,
And they slammed the door tight.

12

"Keep still," said the brothers.
"Be quiet, and hide!"
"Why hide?" said their sister,
"You should all go outside."

"You can't spend your whole life
Just sitting and quaking.
There are places to see
And things to be making."

"Keep the door shut!"
The three brothers cried.
"We're safe in here, Sister.
We won't go outside."

"You're hopeless!" their sister
Cried out with a frown.
Then she huffed and she puffed
And she blew their house down!

As soon as the dust
Had started to clear,
Pig Four said, "You see,
There are no wolves out here."

The boys peeked over
What was left of their wall.
There were no wolves in sight—
There were no wolves at all!

"Hooray!" cried the brothers.
"How happy are we!
For the wolves are all gone,
And now we are free."

20

"We won't spend our whole lives
Just sitting and quaking.
There are places to see
And things to be making!"

21

The boys got some fudge.
Then they built a canoe.
Then they climbed up a mountain
To look at the view.

And their sister, Pig Four,
Traveled out to explore
The wide world that's out there—
Beyond the front door.